ANOTHER SQUIGGLY STORY

This book is dedicated to young writers everywhere. Tell your story! It matters. — A.L.

To Rick L. — M.L.

Text © 2022 Andrew Larsen
Illustrations © 2022 Mike Lowery

Published in Canada and the U.S. by Kids Can Press Ltd.
25 Dockside Drive, Toronto, ON M5A 0B5

Kids Can Press is a Corus Entertainment Inc. company

www.kidscanpress.com

The artwork in this book was rendered in Photoshop.
The text is set in Italo Light and Haneda Semi Bold.

Edited by Yvette Ghione and Debbie Rogosin
Designed by Karen Powers

Printed and bound in Shenzhen, China,
in 10/2021 by Imago
CM 22 0 9 8 7 6 5 4 3 2 1

LIBRARY AND ARCHIVES CANADA CATALOGUING IN PUBLICATION

Title: Another squiggly story / by Me (and Andrew Larsen) ; illustrated by Me (and Mike Lowery).

Names: Larsen, Andrew, 1960– author. | Lowery, Mike, 1980– illustrator.

Identifiers: Canadiana 20210277203 | ISBN 9781525304828 (hardcover)

Classification: LCC PS8623.A77 A83 2022 | DDC jC813/.6 — dc23

Kids Can Press gratefully acknowledges that the land on which our office is located is the traditional territory of many nations, including the Mississaugas of the Credit, the Anishnabeg, the Chippewa, the Haudenosaunee and the Wendat peoples, and is now home to many diverse First Nations, Inuit and Métis peoples.

We thank the Government of Ontario, through Ontario Creates; the Ontario Arts Council; the Canada Council for the Arts; and the Government of Canada for supporting our publishing activity.

ANOTHER SQUIGGLY STORY

BY **ME**
(AND ANDREW LARSEN)

ILLUSTRATED BY **ME**
(AND MIKE LOWERY)

KIDS CAN PRESS

BUT THE SOUND OF MR. LOPEZ'S VOICE ALWAYS BRINGS ME BACK DOWN TO EARTH.

This weekend, I want you to think about the things that MAKE YOU WHO YOU ARE.

Next week, you'll be writing stories about YOURSELVES.

HOW AM I GOING TO DO THAT?

"YOU JUST GAVE ME AN IDEA!" I TELL HER.
"I'M GOING TO CALL MY STORY
THE STORY OF ME BY ME!"

"I LIKE IT!"
SAYS MY SISTER.

"IT'S CATCHY."

WHAT'S THE STORY OF ME?

MARCUS IS GOING TO WRITE ABOUT

H A T S.

ALIA IS GOING TO WRITE ABOUT

VAMPIRES.

WHAT AM I GOING TO WRITE ABOUT?
MAYBE I'LL START WITH THE TITLE.

"DID YOU THINK ABOUT YOUR STORIES OVER THE WEEKEND?" MR. LOPEZ ASKS ON MONDAY.

"I DREW A PICTURE OF MY **CAT**," JAMES SAYS.

I'm going to write a story about the day we brought her home from the cat rescue.

Does your cat have fangs? Is she a VAMPIRE cat?

NO. She's a kitty cat.

"I'M GOING TO DRAW **HATS** ON EVERY PAGE OF MY STORY," SAYS MARCUS.

"I THOUGHT OF A **TITLE**," I SAY.

The STORY of ME by ME.

CATCHY! That's good.

"LET'S BRAINSTORM,"

SAYS MR. LOPEZ.

We're going to pair up and talk about our IDEAS.
It will help us get ready to write our stories.

I LOOK AT MARCUS AND MARCUS LOOKS AT ME.
WE'RE ALWAYS PARTNERS.

I need something to write about.

I need a title.

At least you have your hats.

MY HATS? That's it! I'll call my story MY HATS! THANKS!

No problem.
But what about ME?
What am I going
to write about?

I like my hats.
James likes his cat.
Alia likes vampires.
What do YOU like?

I LIKE LOTS OF THINGS, BUT I STILL DON'T KNOW
WHAT TO WRITE. SO, I KEEP THINKING.

Hmmm.

Time to start your FIRST DRAFTS.

They aren't supposed to be perfect. Just put something on the page. ANYTHING.

I CAN DO THAT.
I'LL MAKE A LIST, LIKE MY SISTER DOES.
I THINK OF THINGS I LIKE, LIKE MARCUS SAID.

I KEEP GOING.

THINGS I KNOW

- The DIFFERENCE between the big dipper and the Little dipper
- How to find the NORTH STAR
- FACTS about MARS
- the difference between a great white shark AND A HAMMERHEAD

THINGS I WANT to be

- an astronaut
- An astronomer
- A marine biologist
- TALL!

THREE LISTS!

THAT WAS EASY.
BUT DO LISTS
MAKE A STORY?

WHEN WE GET BACK FROM THE PARK,
I TAKE A LOOK AT MY LISTS.
I LOOK FOR CONNECTIONS.

LIKE WHEN I LOOK AT THE SKY
AT NIGHT AND TRY TO CONNECT
THE STARS, LIKE CONNECT-THE-DOTS.

THAT'S HOW I SPOT THE
BIG DIPPER.

Hmmm.

IF I CONNECT THE DOTS
BETWEEN MY LISTS,
MAYBE I'LL SEE SOMETHING.

MAYBE IT WILL BE A STORY.

"DRAWING IS EASIER THAN WRITING FOR ME," SAYS MARCUS.

I like the way you drew all those HATS on your cover.

My story is going to be like a comic. Those are the kinds of books I like to read. So that's the kind of story I want to write.

I TAKE ANOTHER LOOK AT MY LISTS ...

I ADD ONE MORE THING.

AND THEN I GO BACK TO THINKING.